D1450636

A Note to Parents and Caregivers:

Read-it! Readers are for children who are just starting on the amazing road to reading. These beautiful books support both the acquisition of reading skills and the love of books.

The PURPLE LEVEL presents basic topics and objects using high frequency words and simple language patterns.

The RED LEVEL presents familiar topics using common words and repeating sentence patterns.

The BLUE LEVEL presents new ideas using a larger vocabulary and varied sentence structure.

The YELLOW LEVEL presents more challenging ideas, a broad vocabulary, and wide variety in sentence structure.

The GREEN LEVEL presents more complex ideas, an extended vocabulary range, and expanded language structures.

The ORANGE LEVEL presents a wide range of ideas and concepts using challenging vocabulary and complex language structures.

When sharing a book with your child, read in short stretches, pausing often to talk about the pictures. Have your child turn the pages and point to the pictures and familiar words. And be sure to reread favorite stories or parts of stories.

There is no right or wrong way to share books with children. Find time to read with your child, and pass on the legacy of literacy.

Adria F. Klein, Ph.D.
Professor Emeritus
California State University
San Bernardino, California

Editor: Jill Kalz
Designer: Nathan Gassman
Colorist: James Mackey
Page Production: Melissa Kes
Associate Managing Editor: Christianne Jones
The illustrations in this book were created with watercolor.

Picture Window Books
5115 Excelsior Boulevard
Suite 232
Minneapolis, MN 55416
877-845-8392
www.picturewindowbooks.com

Printed in the United States of America.

Library of Congress Cataloging-in-Publication Data
Williams, Jacklyn.
Make a new friend, Gus! / by Jacklyn Williams ; illustrated by Doug Cushman.
p. cm. — (Read-it! readers. Gus the hedgehog)
Summary: When Bean makes friends with Sam, who just moved into the
neighborhood, Gus becomes jealous and will not have anything to do with them.
ISBN-13: 978-1-4048-2711-0 (hardcover)
ISBN-10: 1-4048-2711-0 (hardcover)
[1. Best friends—Fiction. 2. Friendship—Fiction. 3. Hedgehogs—Fiction.] I.
Cushman, Doug, ill. II. Title. III. Series.
PZ7.W6656Mak 2006
[E]—dc22   2006003382

Make a New Friend, Gus!

by Jacklyn Williams
illustrated by Doug Cushman

Special thanks to our advisers for their expertise:

Adria F. Klein, Ph.D.
Professor Emeritus, California State University
San Bernardino, California

Susan Kesselring, M.A.
Literacy Educator
Rosemount–Apple Valley–Eagan (Minnesota) School District

PiCTURE WiNDOW BOOKS
Minneapolis, Minnesota

"It's your turn to push the cattle, partner," Gus said to Bean in his best cowboy voice. "Now get a move on."

But just as Bean started to push, a moving van stopped at the house next door.

"The new neighbors are here!" Bean shouted.

Gus tipped back his hat to look.

"My mom said they have a kid our age," said Bean. "It'll be fun to have a new friend."

Gus looked worried. "Do you think we have room for another cowboy?" he asked.

"Sure," said Bean. "Let's go over there and say howdy."

"No, you go ahead. I have to herd these cattle," Gus said.

"OK," said Bean. "But if you change your mind, I'll be at the new kid's house."

The next morning, Gus went to Bean's house, but Bean wasn't there.

"That's strange," thought Gus. "Bean never goes anywhere without me."

Just then, Gus heard a shriek. It came from the new kid's backyard. Gus ran across the street to check it out.

"You're it, Sam!" laughed Bean.

Bean and the new kid were having so much fun that they didn't even notice Gus. To make matters worse, the new kid was ... a GIRL!

The following day, Bean and Sam built a bike
jump together. Gus watched from behind a tree.

"I guess Bean's too busy now to be my friend,"
said Gus.

Gus shuffled across the street and into his house. He flopped down on his bed.

"Well, who needs them? I wouldn't play with them if they asked me a MILLION BILLION times!" Gus said.

On Monday, Bean and Sam asked Gus to sit with them at lunch.

Gus sat at a table across the room.

On Tuesday, Bean and Sam asked Gus to swing with them.

Gus played on the slide.

On Wednesday, Bean and Sam asked Gus to be on their softball team.

Gus played for the other side.

On Thursday, Bean and Sam asked Gus if he
wanted to be first in line at the drinking fountain.

Gus marched to the end of the line.

On Friday, Bean and Sam asked Gus to walk home with them after school.

Gus rode the bus.

Whenever Bean asked Gus what was wrong,
Gus answered, "Nothing."

"Sam really wants to be your friend," Bean said.

Gus looked away.

"Remember, Gus," Bean said. "You and I didn't know each other at first either. Now we're best friends! There's always room for a new friend."

After breakfast on Saturday, Gus went out to play. First, he lined up his cattle. Then he practiced lassoing them. But it wasn't any fun. "I wish Bean was here," Gus said.

Suddenly, a voice yelled, "HELP ME! SOMEBODY, HELP ME!"

"It sounds like Bean and the new kid are having fun without me again," said Gus.

"HELP ME! WON'T SOMEBODY PLEASE HELP ME?" cried the voice again.

"Wait a minute," said Gus. "That doesn't sound like somebody having fun." He ran and looked over the fence into the new kid's backyard. Nobody was there.

"Up here!" cried the voice.

There, in the tallest tree in the yard, stood a tree house. In the doorway of the tree house stood Sam.

"The ladder broke, and I can't get down," she said. "Would you please help me?"

Gus scrambled over the fence and tossed the rope up to Sam. She tied it around a branch and climbed down.

"Thank you," said Sam. "Thank you a MILLION BILLION times. My name's Sam."

Gus tipped back his hat and smiled. "And I'm Gus," he said in his best cowboy voice.

"Let's go find Bean," Gus continued. "We're going to need help herding the cattle."

"You mean, I can help, too?" asked Sam.

"Of course," said Gus. "There's always room for a new friend!"

More *Read-it!* Readers

Bright pictures and fun stories help you practice your reading skills. Look for more books at your level.

Happy Birthday, Gus! 1-4048-0957-0

Happy Easter, Gus! 1-4048-0959-7

Happy Halloween, Gus! 1-4048-0960-0

Happy Thanksgiving, Gus! 1-4048-0961-9

Happy Valentine's Day, Gus! 1-4048-0962-7

Let's Go Fishing, Gus! 1-4048-2713-7

Matt Goes to Mars 1-4048-1269-5

Merry Christmas, Gus! 1-4048-0958-9

Pick a Pet, Gus! 1-4048-2712-9

Rumble Meets Buddy Beaver 1-4048-1287-3

Rumble Meets Chester the Chef 1-4048-1335-7

Rumble Meets Eli Elephant 1-4048-1332-2

Rumble Meets Keesha Kangaroo 1-4048-1290-3

Rumble Meets Milly the Maid 1-4048-1341-1

Rumble Meets Penny Panther 1-4048-1331-4

Rumble Meets Sylvia and Sally Swan 1-4048-1541-4

Rumble Meets Wally Warthog 1-4048-1289-X

Welcome to Third Grade, Gus! 1-4048-2714-5

Looking for a specific title or level? A complete list of *Read-it!* Readers is available on our Web site:

www.picturewindowbooks.com